CHI CHI THE RESCUE DOG
NEVER GIVE UP

Elizabeth Howell

Illustrated by Blayne Fox

BROWN BOOKS KIDS

NEVER GIVE UP

Brown Books Kids
Dallas / New York
www.BrownBooksKids.com
(972) 381-0009

A New Era in Publishing®

Publisher's Cataloging-In-Publication Data

Names: Howell, Elizabeth, 1971- author. | Fox, Blayne, illustrator.
Title: Chi Chi the rescue dog. [1], Never give up / Elizabeth Howell ; illustrated by Blayne Fox.
Other Titles: Never give up
Description: Dallas ; New York : Brown Books Kids, [2021] | Interest age level: 005-008. | Summary: "This is the true story of Chi Chi, an abandoned and severely-injured golden retriever who was rescued, treated, and then adopted and loved by her forever family. She discovers how perseverance and trust in God's will can allow one to make it through so many tough times and see the better side of life"--Provided by publisher.
Identifiers: ISBN 9781612545332
Subjects: LCSH: Dog rescue--Juvenile literature. | Golden retriever--Wounds and injuries--Juvenile literature. | Perseverance (Ethics)--Juvenile literature. | Trust in God--Juvenile literature. | CYAC: Dog rescue. | Golden retriever--Wounds and injuries. | Perseverance (Ethics) | Trust in God.
Classification: LCC SF426.5 .H68 2021 | DDC 636.70832--dc23

This book has been officially leveled by using the
F&P Text Level Gradient™ Leveling System.

ISBN 978-1-61254-533-2
LCCN 2021908347

Printed in Canada
10 9 8 7 6 5 4 3 2 1

For more information or to contact the author, please go to
www.ChiChiRescueDog.com.

DEDICATION

To Chi Chi, the most extraordinary dog I have ever loved. You are a very special gift from God, and your courage, determination, joy, and ability to never give up inspire me every day.

ACKNOWLEDGMENTS

I would like to thank my husband, Richard, and my daughter, Megan, for agreeing to adopt a quadruple amputee dog from the other side of the world that I had fallen in love with. Giving Chi Chi the best life possible has made all of our lives better. I would also like to thank my family and friends for their support and encouragement, especially my parents. Their input on the book and their fostering of my passion for helping animals has been a gift.

To all of the amazing people that have contributed to Chi Chi's story in so many different ways, I thank you for everything you have done for my sweet girl: Juyun Yu, Cody Yoshizawa and the Nabiya Irion Hope Project team, Dr. Lee and the veterinarians and nurses at the Irion Animal Hospital in South Korea, Shannon Keith, Monique Hanson and the Beagle Freedom Project team, Dr. Valerie Ferguson, Lynn Parkhurst and the Four Legged Friends Animal Hospital team, Derrick Campana and the Bionic Pets team, Ron and Rosemary Goldstein and the Arizona Prosthetic Orthotic Services team, Jeffrey and Karen Flocker of Canine Physical Rehabilitation of the Southwest, and all of Chi Chi's social media friends around the world. I would also like to thank my editor, my illustrator, and the team at Brown Books.

Most importantly, I would like to thank God for bringing Chi Chi into my life and for providing a way for me to share her story with the world. May Chi Chi's life and this book bring glory to God.

A NOTE FROM THE AUTHOR

There are thousands of amazing rescue animals waiting to be adopted. Rescue animals have often been abused, neglected, or abandoned. Animals like Chi Chi with special needs are even less likely to be adopted. We hope that you will consider adopting a rescue animal as your next pet. You can find rescue groups and shelters in your area by searching online.

Chi Chi the Golden Retriever was friends with all of the dogs at the kennel. *Snuggling with my friends is comforting,* Chi Chi thought.

There wasn't enough room
to play inside the kennel.

*I wish we could go outside. Then we
could play ball, or run and play chase.*

Then one day, Chi Chi woke up outside the kennel.
She had wanted to go outside, but not like this.
Chi Chi's legs were injured. She couldn't walk.

안개잦은지역
(1km 앞)
운행주의
비상등을 켬시다

A mean man had stolen Chi Chi from the kennel. He hurt
her and then abandoned her. Chi Chi looked all around.
Where are my friends?

Soon, some compassionate people rescued Chi Chi. "Don't give up, sweet girl. We will help you and get you the care you need." They drove her to the animal hospital.

Chi Chi nodded.

Thank you.

At the animal hospital, the doctors and nurses cared for Chi Chi.

"You will get better after I remove the parts of your legs that are injured beyond repair," the doctor said.

Will I be able to play again? Chi Chi wondered.
I have to be brave and NEVER GIVE UP.

My legs look different now, but I feel better, and this blanket is purple, my favorite color.

"Chi Chi, you're an amputee now. You need to rest so your legs can heal. Then, you will need to learn to walk again," the doctor said.

Who will help me? I miss my old friends.

"Chi Chi, you can play with this toy while you are getting better," the doctor said.

Chi Chi smiled and snuggled close to the toy. *I'll name you Ellie.*

Chi Chi liked making new dog friends at the hospital. But all too soon, they went home with their families. Chi Chi was a rescue dog now. She needed a loving family to adopt her.

I want a forever family so I can make new dog friends that I can play with all the time.

Chi Chi knew that God had a special plan for her. *I have to be brave and NEVER GIVE UP.*

Day after day, Chi Chi worked hard to get stronger. *I want to walk again.*

One day, all of her hard work paid off.

Look at me! I'm walking!

The vets were cheering, "You're amazing!" Now, Chi Chi could leave the hospital and join the forever family that had adopted her.

Will my new forever family be able to take care of me? Chi Chi wondered. *Will I make new dog friends?* Chi Chi snuggled Ellie to help her feel brave.

When the car stopped, the back door opened. Chi Chi and Ellie looked out at their new forever family in the front yard. *Everyone looks friendly, and there are three dog friends, too!*

Daddy reached into the back seat and picked up Chi Chi and Ellie. "I will carry you when you need help."

"We will protect you," Mommy said. "No one will ever hurt you again."

"You are safe now," said Megan.

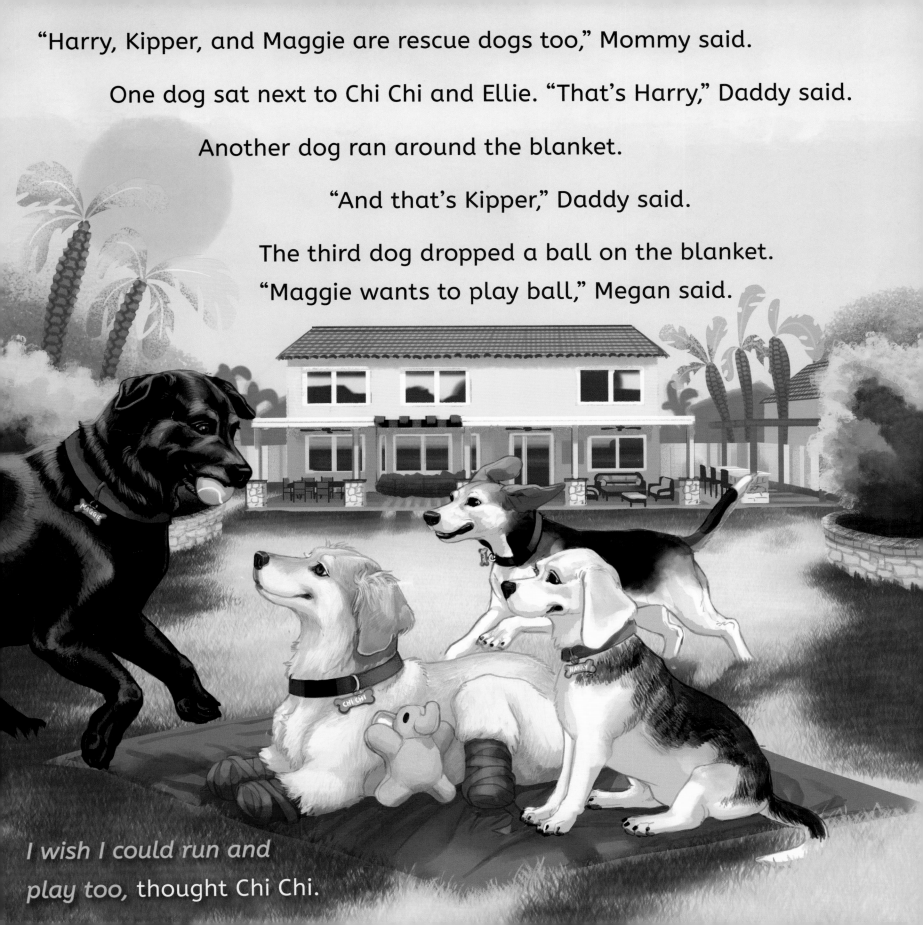

"Harry, Kipper, and Maggie are rescue dogs too," Mommy said.

One dog sat next to Chi Chi and Ellie. "That's Harry," Daddy said.

Another dog ran around the blanket.

"And that's Kipper," Daddy said.

The third dog dropped a ball on the blanket.
"Maggie wants to play ball," Megan said.

I wish I could run and play too, thought Chi Chi.

Chi Chi's forever family loved her and took very good care of her. "Chi Chi, we need to bandage your legs every morning so you can walk," Mommy said.

Chi Chi nodded. *Thank you.*

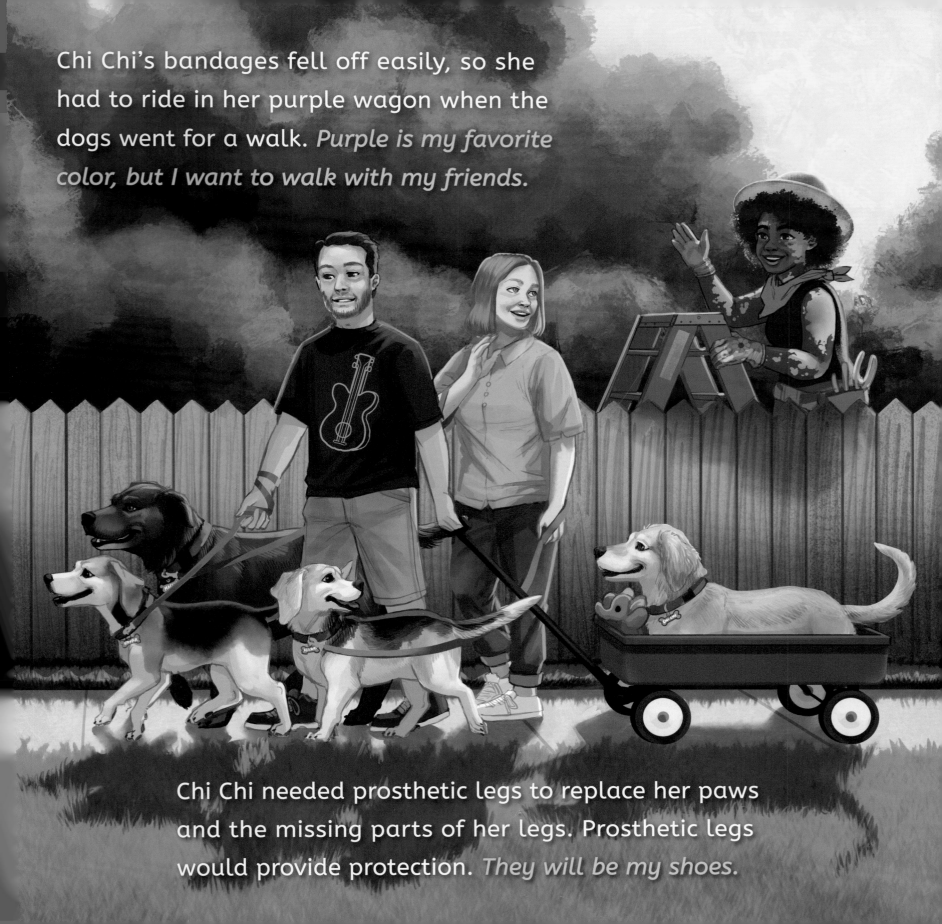

Chi Chi's bandages fell off easily, so she had to ride in her purple wagon when the dogs went for a walk. *Purple is my favorite color, but I want to walk with my friends.*

Chi Chi needed prosthetic legs to replace her paws and the missing parts of her legs. Prosthetic legs would provide protection. *They will be my shoes.*

Wait for me! Chi Chi wanted to go up the stairs, just like her friends.

I need to work hard and get stronger so I can get my shoes and go up the stairs all by myself.

I can't do everything that my friends can do, but my forever family is always there to help and encourage me. I will remain joyful and never give up.

Chi Chi didn't need shoes to snuggle with Ellie and Mommy.

I love snuggling. Mommy tells me that I'm brave and can do anything if I work hard and don't give up. She reminds me that even though this is really difficult, God has a special plan for me.

Mommy took Chi Chi to rehab. Dogs
that are injured swim to get better.
I always bring Ellie. She makes rehab fun.

Chi Chi swam in the water and fetched Ellie.

I have to work hard and get stronger. I want to get my shoes so I can play like my friends.

When she was strong enough, Chi Chi went to the vet to get fitted for her shoes. "When your new shoes arrive, you will be able to run and play with your friends!" the vet said.

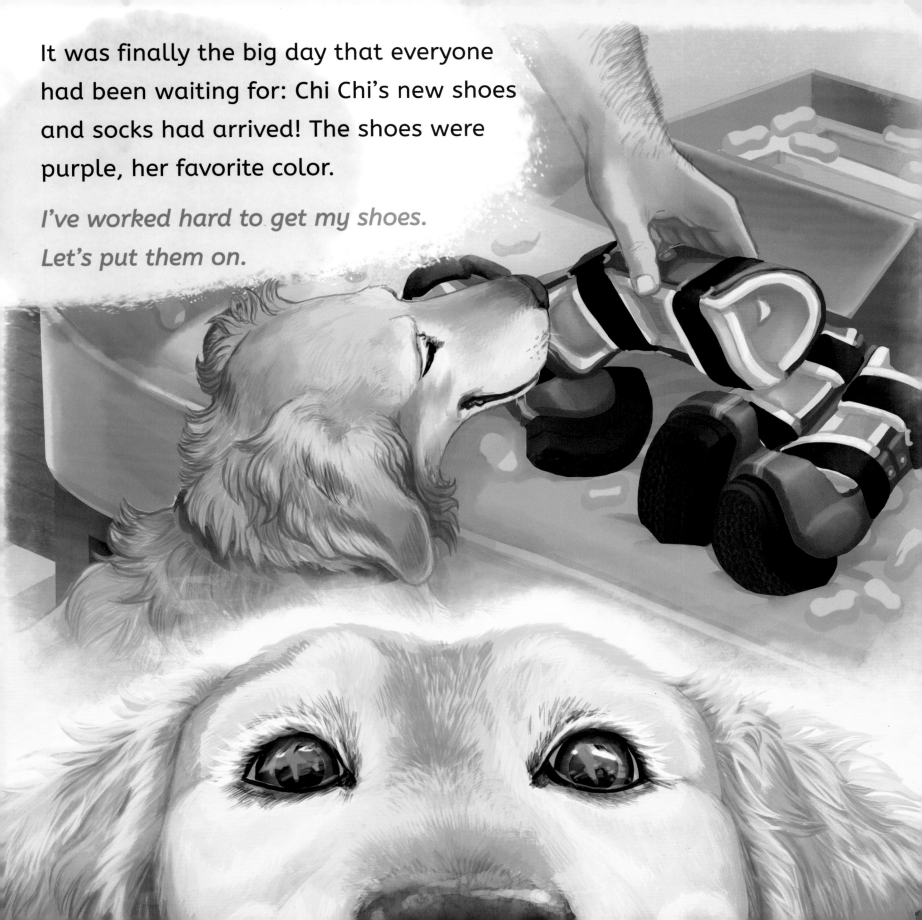

It was finally the big day that everyone had been waiting for: Chi Chi's new shoes and socks had arrived! The shoes were purple, her favorite color.

I've worked hard to get my shoes.
Let's put them on.

Chi Chi didn't need the wagon anymore. That afternoon, she went for a walk with Maggie, Kipper, and Harry. *I love exploring all of the sights and smells up close.*

When Chi Chi wore her shoes, she could run and play just like her friends.

Even though my legs look different, now I can do the same things that my dog friends can do.

I don't need paws. When I wear my shoes, I can go up the stairs just like Maggie, Kipper, and Harry.

God really did have a special plan for me. My joy enabled me to NEVER GIVE UP. My dream of having a loving forever family came true.

What other amazing things does God have planned for me?

ABOUT THE AUTHOR

Elizabeth Howell has been passionate about helping animals since she was a child. This book is based on the true story of a golden retriever that her family adopted named Chi Chi. Elizabeth hopes that everyone that reads this book will be inspired by Chi Chi's ability to never give up and be joyful, regardless of her circumstances.

Chi Chi was rescued after being found in a trash bag with her legs bound. Due to the severity of her injuries, the only way to save her life was to amputate portions of all four of her legs. When she was healthy enough to travel, she was adopted by the Howell family in Phoenix, Arizona. Chi Chi's incredible story has been featured by Animal Planet, The Dodo, American Humane, *The Today Show, People, Modern Dog Magazine, Woman's World*, the *Washington Post*, and more.

You can learn more about Chi Chi's extraordinary story and the Howell family's other rescue dogs at:

www.ChiChiRescueDog.com
Social Media: @chichirescuedog

ABOUT THE ILLUSTRATOR

Illustrator Blayne Fox, a child of the Midwestern United States, grew up romping through the Missouri woodlands, indulging her imagination with the magical kingdoms and creatures inspired by native flora and fauna. Predominantly self-taught, Blayne knew what she was going to be from a very young age: an illustrator. After attending art college, she plunged into her industry, working for clients such as Discovery Channel and *National Geographic Kids* within her first year out of school. She primarily focuses on illustrating children's books and graphic novels.